# The Timid Frog

Written by Catherine Veitch Illustrated by Amanda Enright

Miles Kelly

All the nocturnal animals were waking up for the evening.

"Eek! What's that?" Fae the giant tree frog was afraid of everything that moved.

Now that she was no longer a tadpole and had grown up, it was time for Fae to leave her forest pool. Her brothers and sisters had already left to live in the trees.

It felt strange standing on land with her new legs for the first time.

Nervously Fae hopped across the leafy forest floor onto a fallen branch.

"Hey, watch out!" said Lara a leaf-tailed gecko. "You're hopping on my tail!"

Fae asked Lara if she had seen her family.

"I saw some frogs hopping that way," said Lara. "But watch out for a wild pig who eats frogs like you."

Honk! Squeal!

Suddenly there was loud honk! and squeal! Fae remembered Lara's warning and darted inside a hollow log just in time. A wild pig charged past, making Fae tremble.

When the pig had gone, Fae crept out of her hiding place. She wished that she could return to her forest pool where she felt safe and happy.

"He...lllooooo!" echoed the log behind Fae. She sprang round to face whatever had been hiding in the log with her.

"Who's there?" she asked shyly.

"Sorry I startled you. I'm Beau, a bandicoot."

Fae and Beau climbed onto the log and laughed at what a scaredy-cat Fae had been.

"I saw some frogs climbing that tree," said Beau.

Fae was hopeful that she would soon see her family.

Fae stood at the bottom of a huge tree that seemed to go on forever. It had been raining and the trunk was wet and slippery.

"How can I climb that?" she whispered to herself.

Fae took a deep breath and leapt onto the trunk.

Climbing the tree was
easier than she thought.

But Fae was not alone in the tree...

ZZZZZZZZZZZZZZZZZZZZZZZZZZZZZZZZ

Above Fae, and blocking her path, was a huge, sleeping frilled lizard! Fae did not know if the lizard was friendly, but she wasn't hanging around to find out!

There was no way round the snoozing lizard so Fae would have to do a huge hop over it.

"One, two, three," she counted, and then...

ZZZZZ
Hop!

...Fae leapt magnificently over the lizard, but landed right in front of a dozing green tree python!

"Argh!" gasped Fae. Her big brother had often frightened her with stories of snakes that gobbled up frogs. Luckily, this snake had just eaten and was fast asleep. But Fae certainly didn't want to wake him!

"Pssst," whispered a voice that made Fae jump. She looked up. Two bright eyes belonging to a spotted cuscus stared from between the leaves. "Hop up the vine," the cuscus said.

"Thanks," replied Fae. She was glad to leave the snake behind.

"I'm Cooper," said the cuscus.

Cooper said that some frogs had passed him just yesterday, and told Fae to follow him.

But Cooper was not the quickest animal in the rainforest! He climbed so slowly that Fae could not wait a minute longer. She sprang over Cooper, zipped along the branch and bashed into...

...Freya the flying fox.

"Who do we have here?" asked Freya between mouthfuls of fruit.

"Don't worry," gulped Fae. "I'm not hanging around," and she hopped past Freya as fast as she could.

Next Fae met Sofia the sugar glider who had some bad news.

"Some green-eyed tree frogs live in THIS tree, but a family of giant tree frogs live over in THAT tree," said Sofia.

Fae had climbed the wrong tree!

"I can't jump to that tree from here," she wept.

"I have an idea," replied Sofia.

Sofia told Fae to climb onto her back.
Fae clung on tight and screamed as they
glided through the air. **Thwack!**

They had made it! Fae's brothers and sisters were there and she could not wait to tell them all about her journey.

"I can't believe how brave you are now," said Flyn, Fae's eldest brother.

Fae smiled at Flyn and said, "Yes, I am brave!"

The
End